This Book Belongs To:

_____

COUNTDOWN
TO
CHRISTMAS

Illustrated by
Joe Boddy

Rhymes by
Katie Campbell

The Unicorn Publishing House, Inc.
Morris Plains, New Jersey

1
One is for Santa,
Jolly old Saint Nick,
Sound asleep by his sleigh.
Awaken him quick!

2 Two are his boots
To carry him off.
Time to get up,
Time to be off!

3 Three are his clothes—
Red coat, pants, and cap.
With a yawn and a stretch,
Santa wakes from his nap.

4 Four are the blankets
To keep Santa warm,
As he rides in his sleigh
Before Christmas dawns.

5

Five are the sacks
Piled high in the sleigh.
Can you find five teddy bears
Hidden away?

6 Six are the turkeys,
Brought for the feast.
A merry Christmas dinner
For all to sit and eat.

7
Seven are the doors—
Seven from which to choose.
Which door could be big enough;
Which door will they use?

8 Eight are Santa's reindeer
Ready for their flight.
How does Santa know their names
When they look so much alike?

9 Nine are Santa's elves
Who make toys day and night.
They gather quickly round the sleigh
As Santa starts his flight.

10 Ten are tiny stars
Twinkling in the sky,
Guiding Santa from the North.
How many can you spy?

11 Eleven are the chimneys
That come in Santa's view.
Eleven are the tiny homes,
Can you count them, too?

12 Twelve are the steps
Left by Santa's boots;
Twelve frosty frozen footprints
Tracked across the roof.

13

Thirteen are the family
Snoring fast asleep.
Thirteen happy dreamers
As Santa brings them treats.

14 Fourteen are the presents
Placed beneath the tree.
Fourteen gifts are given—
Left on Christmas Eve.

15 Fifteen are the angels,
Halos shining bright,
Hung upon the Christmas tree.
Are they all in sight?

16 Sixteen are the silver bells
That ring out in the night.
Two are worn by each reindeer—
Did I count them right?

17

Seventeen are the signs
For seventeen cities to see.
Jolly Santa will visit them all
But which is the first to be?

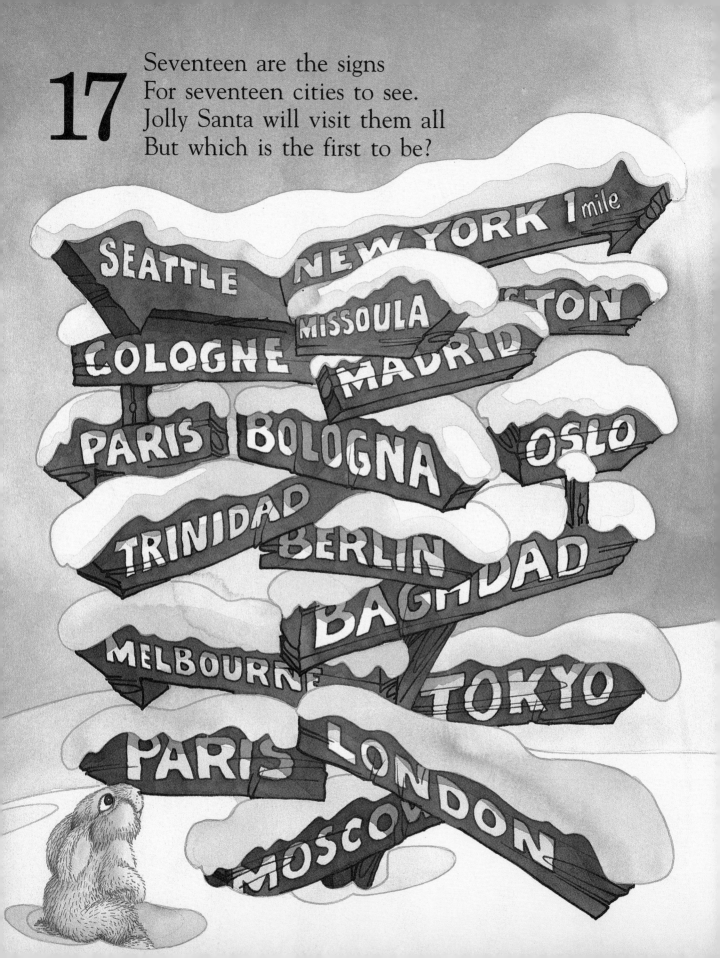

18

Eighteen are the shining rays
Cast by the morning sun
That beckon weary Santa home
When Christmas Eve is done.

19 Nineteen are the snowfilled trees
Over which the reindeer climb.
Now count as quickly as you can
And Santa's home you'll find.

20 Twenty are for Santa's toes
And fingers can't you see.
"A very merry Christmas,"
Santa says, "to you, little one, from me!"